MW00907356

MIMI'S GIFT

Joan M. Thomas

To Lauren,
Work, fellows faith.
Joan M. Thomas,
R.N.
08-21-05

WINEPRESS **WP** PUBLISHING

© 2003 by Joan M. Thomas. All rights reserved.

Packaged by WinePress Publishing, PO Box 428, Enumclaw, WA 98022. The views expressed or implied in this work do not necessarily reflect those of WinePress Publishing. The author is ultimately responsible for the design, content, and editorial accuracy of this work.

Cover illustrated by Joan M. Thomas.
Cover by Ragont Design.

No part of this publication may be reproduced, stored in a retrieval system or transmitted in any way by any means, electronic, mechanical, photocopy, recording or otherwise, without the prior permission of the copyright holder except as provided by USA copyright law.

Unless otherwise noted, all scriptures are taken from the King James Version of the Bible.

ISBN 1-57921-482-7
Library of Congress Catalog Card Number: 2002107419

Dedication

Mimi's Gift is dedicated to my sons, Rick and David; my grandchildren, Sarah, Sean, Christopher, and Daniel; and in memory of my mother, Margaret L. Regal.

And to all who desire to seek God's will, do His work, and live by faith.

"Mimi's Gift is a gift to all who get a chance to share this story with a child they love. It is a story of hope and love, furthering bedrock Christian values and traditions of the Moravian Church. It is a story that transcends time periods of past, present, and future, and focuses on family togetherness and the sharing of stories that should be handed down from generation to generation. It is a gem!"

—Deanna Hollenbach, Director of Communication

Interprovincial Board of Communication

Moravian Church in North America

"This project obviously represents much labor and love on your part. It is wonderful that you have told a meaningful story and also added the illustrations and the music and text of "Mimi's Happy Angel Song."

—Rev. David A. Schattschneider, Ph.D.

Dean and Vice President Emeritus

Moravian Theological Seminary

"I loved this beautiful story. Thank you for letting me read it. I especially liked the message woven through every page—work follows faith."

—Hope MacDonald, Author

Acknowledgements

I sincerely thank my family, friends, and all the people who encouraged and prayed for me and this little fiction story.

My husband, Dick, for his patience and computer help.

My sons, David and Rick, who encouraged me. Dave was always there when computer assistance was needed.

My understanding daughters-in-law, Laura and Carla—Laura for her music scoring.

Sarah and Daniel for their enthusiasm and encouragement.

Deanna Hollenbach, Director of Communication, Interprovincial Board of Communication, Moravian Church in America.

Rev. David A. Schattschneider, Ph.D., Dean and Vice President Emeritus, Moravian Theological Seminary.

Hope MacDonald, Author.

Rev. David M. Dorpat.

Miss Suzanne VinceCruz, B.A.E. in Music, K–8 Elementary Education Certification.

Rev. Walter John Boris.

Members of the Washington Moravian Fellowship.

Table of Contents

Preface

Although Mimi's Gift is a work of fiction, much of it is drawn from my life experiences. Now I am a mother and grandmother, but I remember my Moravian roots and my mother's faith in God. Whenever I faced a challenging situation my mother would say, "Have faith, for this, too, shall pass." My mother taught that good deeds and "Work Follows Faith."

I remember our old trunk and the treasures buried safely inside. Over the years I discovered that the greatest treasure is the gift of faith.

My granddaughter and I are pictured below in our Moravian outfits.

Part One

The Tea Party

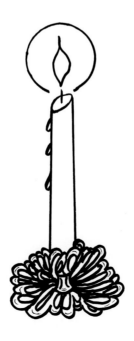

You are invited to a Tea Party

At Grandma's home

December 24th at 3 o'clock.

Please say you'll come and have tea with me.

Love,

Grandma

P.S. Dolls and Teddy Bears of all ages and sizes are welcome.

*T*he day for our Christmas Tea is finally here!" Ruth exclaimed. She sat her doll in Grandma's dining room chair. "Grandma, are we going to have a story after our tea party?"

"There might not be enough time," Grandma said. "The Candlelight Service starts at seven o'clock. And you know how much we love to talk."

Grandma smiled at Ruth and laughed. She lifted her cherished blue and white china dishes off the top shelf of the china closet and stacked them neatly on her large oak dining room table.

"You could tell the story during our tea party," Ruth coaxed. "Please?"

She walked over to Grandma's buffet, counted out two bright red Christmas napkins, and began folding them. "Grandma," Ruth said in a perplexed voice, "I can't decide which I love most, your tea parties or your stories. Actually, today I'd like to do both!"

Mimi's Gift

For the Christmas Tea, Ruth and Grandma had agreed to dress up in their best outfits. Ruth had on her favorite long-sleeved royal blue velvet dress and silver heart-shaped locket. The dress matched the deep blue of her sparkling eyes.

Grandma chose her ivory lace blouse and floor-length, red taffeta skirt. A single strand of pearls and a shiny gold cross on a long, gold chain circled her neck. A green and white-checkered apron protected her "good" clothes.

Grandma bent over and rummaged through the bottom china cabinet drawer, finally taking out a sunflower yellow apron for Ruth. "Look," she said. "I found your special apron. Stand still. I'll tie it for you." Grandma wrapped the bright sunny apron around Ruth's waist and tied it in the back with a large bow.

"Thank you, Grandma," Ruth said. "Well! The story could be about you—when you were my age! Remember, I'm exactly eight and a half years old today!"

The Tea Party

Ruth slipped the folded scarlet napkins through the small holes of the green Christmas tree shaped napkin rings and handed the filled rings to Grandma.

"The red napkins will add a dash of color," Grandma said. "My white lace tablecloth is on the table along with the candles. All we need is a centerpiece."

"I have a great idea!" Ruth said. "We can use your Christmas bouquet and little manger scene." She lifted Grandma's poinsettia and evergreen bouquet and nativity figures off the dining room buffet. Ruth placed the bouquet in the middle of the table between two tall beeswax candles. Directly in front of it she arranged the small figures of Mary, Joseph, and Baby Jesus in His crib.

Grandma loved nativity sets. She owned twelve! Her favorite was the set carved by Great-grandfather Jacob Peter Noble. Grandma told Ruth the Nativity Set was a family heirloom and over a hundred years old.

Mimi's Gift

But Grandma's real passion was her Moravian collection. She had books with fascinating pictures about the early Moravians, videos, dolls, stars, candles, paintings, and interesting handmade artifacts. Every Christmas, Grandma put on her Moravian outfit and invited Ruth's Sunday school class to see her collection, hear the history of the Moravian candle and putz, and enjoy an old-fashioned tea party. Ruth's friends were completely charmed by Grandma's delightful tea parties and enthralled by her inspiring, thrilling stories about the brave Moravian missionaries.

This year Ruth helped Grandma host the tea. Ruth wore the Moravian outfit that Grandma had made for her. Ruth's outfit was identical to Grandma's except for the red ribbons that closed the front of her jacket and matched the ties of her cap. Grandma's ribbons were blue. Lacing Ruth's jacket took Grandma a long time—a whole fifteen minutes. Ruth loved the long, full, flowing skirt. When she walked, the skirt swished, sounding like rustling leaves. It swirled and floated around her when she turned around.

The Tea Party

Ruth put her hands on her hips, tilted her head to the right, and stepped back to admire her creative centerpiece. "How does it look, Grandma?" she asked, wrinkling her forehead.

Grandma clapped her hands and smiled. "Your centerpiece is beautiful! Good work!" She gave Ruth a big hug. "Well, let's see. World War Two was going on when I was a girl and our family learned to be frugal." Grandma filled the teakettle with water and put it on the stove to boil.

"We haven't studied much about that in school," Ruth said frowning.

"It was a challenging and unstable time!" Grandma explained. "Mom taught us to have faith, be thankful for what we had, and work hard. We didn't receive many Christmas presents. But we always had enough of what we needed and some to spare. Most of our gifts were either handmade or useful. Like clothes, shoes, or books."

She adjusted her glasses and wiped her hands on her white linen dish towel. Grandma's bifocals had an annoying habit of slipping down over the bridge of her nose.

Mimi's Gift

"Our tea party is at three o'clock," Ruth said, glancing at the kitchen clock. "Grandma, I think we'll have lots of time for a story before Dad and Mom pick us up for church. My girl doll, Rose, wants to hear your story, too."

Grandma slowly put the dainty teacups in the saucers. She thought for a moment. "Ruth, since you're the guest and today is special, I'll tell you a story about my ninth Christmas while we're having our tea party."

"Thank you, Grandma!" Ruth grinned. "I'll hurry and set the table. We'll need two place settings. One for you and one for me. I'll prop Rose up with one of Grandpa's big stuffed pillows so she can reach the table and I'll share my place setting with her."

"First wash your hands!" Grandma reminded her. "Be sure to use soap."

Ruth turned on the hot water at the kitchen sink and picked up the bar of soap. It was yellow and smelled like lemons. "Did you have tea parties with your Grandmother and doll? Is that why you like tea parties so much?"

The Tea Party

"Yes," Grandma said, chuckling. "Those are good questions." She opened the tea caddy and selected her favorite blend.

"What kind of games did you play?" Ruth asked. She scrubbed her hands with the soft bristled brush.

"Oh, my! Why, your Uncle Matt and I played parlor games like chess. Life was simple. Our family didn't even have a telephone! All our activities were centered around family, church, and school. We didn't have computer games, television, or videos for entertainment. Instead we read books, listened to the radio, or played records on our Victrola. It's amazing what fantastic ideas Matt and I came up with to create inexpensive gifts and to help Dad design our Christmas cards." Grandma laughed as she put the tea caddy back in the cupboard.

"What's a Victrola?" Ruth asked, drying her hands on the red and green Christmas tea towel.

Mimi's Gift

"A Victrola is what we played records on. Records were black, round, bigger than CDs, and had a hole in the middle. Some Victrolas ran by electricity and some you cranked by hand. Like this!" Grandma stooped over and pretended to crank a make-believe handle.

Ruth giggled. She held her hands up to the light for Grandma to inspect. "See. My hands are clean! When I finish setting the table I'll take the teapots out of the china closet for you."

Grandma nodded. She opened her wooden silverware chest and removed the pie server, knives, spoons, and forks. After they set the table, Ruth placed the blue and white teapot, matching sugar bowl and creamer, and her little white china pot on a round, pewter tray. She balanced the tray carefully, holding onto both handles, so the delicate china wouldn't tip and fall. Ruth put the tray on the dining room table.

"Thank you, Ruth." Grandma slipped her hand in the forest green potholder and lifted the boiling teakettle off the stove. "Would you like to take the shoo-fly pie out of the cupboard while I brew my tea and make your hot chocolate?"

Mimi's Gift

"Okay, Grandma. Your shoo-fly pie is my favorite tea party dessert! Actually," she said with a wide grin, "it's my favorite *anytime* dessert!"

"Ruth, you're just like Grandpa! He loves the pie, too, with all that melt-in-your-mouth brown sugar, cinnamon, butter, and molasses."

In the hall the old grandfather clock chimed three o'clock.

"It's time for our tea party!" Ruth shouted. She slid the pie onto the large blue pie plate and ran to open the china closet door. Ruth picked up the little white porcelain tea bell and rang it three times. DING! DING! DING!

Ruth looked at the table, glanced down at her apron, and then up at Grandma. She pointed to the candles and whispered, "Look. We forgot to take our aprons off, put the toasted cheese sandwiches and hot potato salad on the table, and light the candles."

"Oh, my!" Grandma said. She hurried to untie her apron and arrange the sandwiches on a tray. After Ruth hung their aprons in the closet, Grandma lit the candles. Then Ruth and Grandma sat

The Tea Party

down at the table and politely spread their red Christmas napkins on their laps.

"I'll say our Moravian table blessing," Ruth offered. Grandma and Ruth bowed their heads while Ruth prayed.

Afterwards, Grandma said, "Thank you, honey, for saying grace. Now I'll serve your hot chocolate and the food."

Ruth glowed from Grandma's praise. To be called "honey" by Grandma was special. It was like winning a gold medal or receiving a straight-A report card! It was the highest compliment you could receive from her.

Grandma poured Ruth's hot chocolate, served her the salad and sandwiches, and dished up the pie. "You might want to top off your chocolate with a marshmallow or a dab of whipped cream," she suggested, smiling.

Mimi's Gift

"Good idea, Grandma! I think I'll have both. A marshmallow for my chocolate and whipped cream for the pie." Ruth put a dab of whipped cream on her pie and carefully dropped a sugary, snowy white marshmallow into her hot chocolate. She took a big bite of pie, savoring the taste of the sweet, gooey molasses. "I'm ready for the story whenever you are, Grandma."

Grandma removed the green crocheted tea cozy from the steaming teapot. She poured the hot tea, added a dash of cream, and slowly stirred it. Then she settled back comfortably in the chair and sipped her tea. "Umm! Perfect! Now," she said, with a wide, contented smile, "where should I begin?"

"What's the name of the story?" Ruth asked. "It needs to have a title!"

"Let's see, what name shall we give it, hmm? Mimi's Gift," she announced emphatically. "That's what we'll call this story."

The Tea Party

"What's the gift?" Ruth asked, leaning forward in her chair. "Is this a mystery tale?"

"Oh!" Grandma said with a wink. "You'll have to wait and find out."

She put her cup back in the saucer and took off her glasses. Grandma lovingly touched the sparkling gold cross around her neck as she looked out her large dining room window at the softly falling snow. It seemed like she was reminiscing about her past and recalling childhood memories of people and places Ruth never knew.

Then Grandma turned toward Ruth and said, "I remember the question I asked my mom when I was just your age . . ."

Part Two

The Story

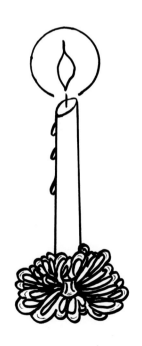

Chapter One
Questions

Whats your favorite holiday, Mom? Christmas is mine! I love Christmas with all the bright decorations, the putz, and our tree." I flung my arms open wide to show her how much I loved it. "And I always know it won't be long until Christmas when we hang our Moravian Star outside."

I buttoned my red flannel nightgown, took off my warm slippers, and climbed into bed. My gown and bathrobe were the color of red holly berries. Downstairs, in the living room our tall grandfather clock chimed nine o'clock.

Every year on the fourth Sunday before Christmas, our family unpacked the storage containers that held the nativity set, Christmas ornaments and lights, and Moravian Star. When Dad put the star together Matt, my older brother, and I counted the points. There were exactly twenty-six!

Mimi's Gift

Matthew was three years older than me. He liked to be called Matt. I couldn't wish for a better big brother. He always stuck up for me and never pulled my pigtails or teased me.

When the star was ready, Matt and I would watch Dad climb up on the stepladder and hang it by our front door. I'd stand in awe as Dad turned the switch on to light it.

"Ooh! Look!" I'd shout and clap my hands as the brilliant light from the star flooded the porch. "Come and see the star, Mom! It's beautiful!"

Dad left the star up until we took our Christmas tree down, and the nativity set and ornaments were packed away.

"Christmas is my favorite holiday, too, Mimi," Mom said, smiling. She smoothed my white flannel sheets and fluffed up my pillow with her work-worn hands. "Remember, though, there won't be many presents." Mom told us we would have to make all our gifts because of Dad starting a new job, the War, and our recent move to Bethlehem.

Matt said he might do wood carvings for his gifts. He liked to whittle. Grandpa Noble was teaching him the art of woodcarving and how to make Moravian Stars, just like Grandmother Noble was teaching me how to dip and mold beeswax candles.

Questions

Mom taught me to crochet, embroider, and knit. That Christmas, I knitted wool mittens for everyone in our family. Each pair was a different color. Hunter green for Dad, navy blue for Matt, and a soft pretty shell pink for Mom. I crocheted red and green placemats and made matching napkin holders for Grandmother and Grandpa. For my cousins, I designed felt hand and finger puppets.

After I wrapped my gifts in red Christmas paper, I put them in a brown paper bag on the top shelf of my closet. The gifts were my secret! I pinned a note on the bag just in case someone looked on the shelf. It said, "PLEASE DO NOT OPEN!" Even knowing there would be few presents could not dampen my enthusiasm!

"Mom, it's exciting to hang the star and trim the tree," I said. "But the best part is building the putz." I loved arranging the small figures of Mary, Joseph, and Baby Jesus in His crib on bits of straw in their wooden stable.

"Do you remember the year you lost Baby Jesus?" Mom asked, laughing heartily.

Mimi's Gift

"Yes. I felt awful! I cried for three days until I found Him under the living room couch."

Matt and I spent our December evenings constructing the putz on a piece of plywood that Dad laid on the floor under our Christmas tree. After Mom covered the plywood with a white sheet, we placed small wooden houses on the covered plywood, to represent the town of Bethlehem. On one side of the Holy Family we stood three Wisemen and their camels; and on the other side we put three shepherds, four sheep, two cows, and a donkey. Dad and Matt shaped the snow-capped mountains surrounding the miniature town out of evergreens, twigs, rocks, moss, and cotton.

"Mom, what do you like best about Christmas?" I asked as she carefully put my slippers by the side of my bed.

"That's a hard question. We have so many lovely customs and traditions." Mom pushed a strand of her wavy graying hair behind her ear. Her face took on a thoughtful look.

Mimi's Gift

Finally Mom answered with a big smile, "I think being with our family and friends at the Candlelight Service would be at the top of my list."

All our relatives lived over thirty miles away. We didn't see them as much as we liked. Sometimes I got to sleep over at Grandmother and Grandpa's house. Staying with them was fun. Grandmother let me sleep in the guest room in her high, old-fashioned canopy bed and she always made Moravian sugar cake for breakfast! I named Grandmother's guest room "The Angel Room" because she had pictures of angels on every wall.

In a serious voice Mom added, "Christmas is a busy time. Getting ready for the holidays demands lots of preparation and work." She counted the chores on her fingers. "Our first task is to hang the star, then design and mail our cards, cut down and decorate the tree, make gifts for family and friends, mold beeswax candles, pick the holly and the evergreens for the advent wreath, do the baking and—"

Questions

"Mom, please stop!" I said, grinning mischievously and waving my arms. "Excuse me for interrupting. But don't forget to include what I like most—building the putz. And besides, we've done almost everything on your list."

Mom laughed and shook her head. She gave me a gentle hug. "Mimi, sometimes you can be quite a tease! You remind me of Grandpa! You have his same dancing, dark eyes and dramatic flare!"

Mom handed me my doll, Patience, and my teddy bear. He didn't have any patches when Dad and Mom gave him to me on my third birthday. But over the years, my teddy bear had lost some of his stuffing and brown fuzzy fur. Mom and I mended him with chestnut colored wool and ebony cotton patches.

Patience was my cloth, girl doll. She had a round, pretty face with big, dark brown eyes, a happy smile, and brown pigtails. That year, when Mom sewed my Moravian outfit, she also made my doll. Mom dressed her in a chocolate brown wool, Moravian outfit exactly like mine. Her little

Mimi's Gift

jacket laced down the front with shiny satin red ribbons that matched her hair bows and the ties in her dainty white linen cap. Tied around her waist was a white linen apron. On her feet were small, black, laced boots. A tiny white Bible was tucked into the saddle brown leather pouch that hung from her arm.

I loved the doll the minute I saw her and named her Patience. *Because*, I thought, *I might actually learn to be more patient if I named her after the trait that I lacked the most.*

I had fun having tea parties and playing paper dolls and dress-up with Patience. I loved my teddy bear, but he was a boy bear and there were some girl things he didn't understand.

Both Patience and my teddy bear knew my favorite color was red and how much I wanted a red velvet dress for Christmas. I'd never ask Mom and Dad for a velvet dress, though. A pretty Christmas dress was a luxury! And Dad said if there was any extra money it would go to buy War Bonds or to the missions.

Questions

Mom sat down on the bed and untied the red ribbons from my pigtails. I shook my head to loosen the tight braids. My hair tumbled like a waterfall down my back in dark, shimmering waves. Mom gently brushed the tangles and snarls out of my long hair.

"Speaking of chores," she said, "did your Sunday school class help trim the beeswax candles?"

"Yes." I answered. "They're wrapped with red frills. Ready to be given out at the Christmas Eve Service." I gave my teddy bear and Patience a hug and covered them up. "Guess what, Mom? I have the best part in the Christmas Play! My role is to explain the origin of the Moravian candle. Martha is the soloist for Morning Star." Martha was my good friend and in my Sunday school class. She had red hair and freckles.

"That's great!" Mom said. "I'm proud of you. Now, crawl under your covers and stay warm. Dad turned the furnace down. We'll have snow before Christmas Eve if this cold weather continues."

Mimi's Gift

Wise, old Mom-Cat meowed an agreement from her comfortable seat in the rocking chair. She belonged to Mr. Sampson, our mailman. When he delivered mail, Mom-Cat rode either on his shoulder or on top of his brown leather mail pouch, stately and proud. She looked like a queen on her throne.

Everyone adored Mom-Cat. She knew several tricks, but she only performed for an appreciative audience and if she was in the mood. Mr. Sampson was going out of town for the weekend, so he said Mom-Cat could stay with us until Monday.

Mom stood up from my bed, walked to the window, and moved the burning beeswax candle off my windowsill. She placed the candle on my maple dresser where it sent a cheerful glow of light throughout the room.

"Look!" I said, pointing to the window. "Are those ice crystals on the windowpane?"

"Yes," Mom said. "And a harsh draft is coming in, too!" She pulled down the shade and closed the heavy drapes. As far back as I can remember it was our custom to put a lighted beeswax candle in our windows during the month of December. Mom said the candle was a symbol, stating that our family welcomed and showed hospitality to friends and strangers.

"Do you really believe it will snow by Christmas? Don't you think Christmas and snow go together?" I continued on without waiting for her answer. "I can't wait until Christmas Eve! Because our play is right before the Lovefeast and Candlelight Service. At six o'clock! I have my part completely memorized." I hurried on, "My teacher asked me to wear my Moravian dress, white linen apron, and cap."

I said all that in one breath. Sometimes my enthusiasm got me into big trouble! And made it hard for me to be patient. One time my schoolteacher, Mrs. Gray, wrote this in the comment section of my report card: "Mimi is an enthusiastic student and has excellent reading skills. However, she needs to learn to be more patient, control her imagination, and complete designated tasks."

MY MORAVIAN OUTFIT

Mom made my Moravian outfit for me. The skirt (petticoat) and my jacket are made out of warm brown wool.

The cap, shift, neckerchief and apron are fashioned from snowy white linen. My cap ties under my chin with bright red ribbons and matches the ribbon lacing on the front of my jacket.

Questions

Mom unfolded a heavy wool blanket and carefully wrapped it and a hot water bottle around my feet. She covered me up with my patriotic red, white, and blue quilt, right to the tip of my chin.

"Mimi, be patient," she said. "Christmas Eve will be here in no time at all. Yes, a gentle snowfall would be nice. However, if we get a heavy storm there's a possibility of being snowed in. We won't be able to attend church if the roads are closed."

"I don't want to miss being in the play or church. I love the music and the Candlelight Service! Now I hope it doesn't snow at all. Or maybe just a few soft flakes." I lowered my voice and pointed to the calendar on my bedroom wall. "Mom, I'm worried! Christmas Eve is next Friday!"

"Why worry? What's the matter?"

"I don't have an offering to take to church!" I confided. "Everybody in my class is going to take a toy gift. Girls are bringing a toy for a girl and boys a toy for a boy. But we don't have the money to buy a toy at the store." I sighed. "I don't even have a nice dress or a winter coat to wear. Last

Mimi's Gift

year's coat is too small. It comes way above my knees. The sleeves are frayed and too tight!" I frowned. "All the kids will have toys and wear their good clothes, except me."

"What will your class do with the toys?" Mom asked with a concerned voice. She put an extra blanket at the foot of my bed.

"Before the play starts we're going to put our gifts in the Christ Child's crib," I said. "Later the toys will be collected and sent to children in Alaska."

"That's very thoughtful of your class."

"But I feel miserable! I'm upset about not having a gift and having to move here. We used to laugh more and have fun before the War caused us to sell our nice home and move into this small house." I scowled. "Is it selfish and wrong to wish I had an offering to take to church?"

Questions

I took a deep breath and punched my pillow. Tears welled in my eyes. "Mom, I wish I had never heard the word *war*! That one word forced us to move, leave our friends and relatives, and stopped my tap dancing lessons!"

Mom kissed my forehead. She took her handkerchief out of her white apron pocket and wiped the tears gently from my eyes. Even though it was winter, Mom's embroidered handkerchief, trimmed in lace, had the soft scent of summer, lilacs, and roses.

Mom-Cat jumped up on the bed and gazed at me as though she understood exactly how unhappy I felt. She meowed softly, rubbed her wet pink nose gently against my cheek, and tickled me with her long, black whiskers. Then Mom-Cat rolled on her back with her white paws held out straight and meowed loudly. She tried to divert my attention to make me laugh. I patted her head and gave her a weak smile. Without rustling my blankets, Mom-Cat curled into a striped gray and white ball at my feet.

Mimi's Gift

Mom took both my hands in hers and sat on my bed. "No, it's not wrong. I'm proud of you for being kind and unselfish. I know it's difficult to understand. Why do some people have more and others have less? Or why can't we buy brand new things at the store? And when will the War be over?"

"I miss our relatives and friends," I said sadly. "And I miss our old school and my tap dancing lessons. No girls my age live around here. Sometimes I get lonesome."

"Mimi, moving to a new house is hard. So is adjusting to a new school and leaving familiar friends. I know you are struggling with these questions, however it is only God who knows the answers. Have faith, for God's love never changes. The War will end one day and these difficult times will pass! Although finances are scarce and we have had to make sacrifices, we are all together."

"I am happy Dad is home," I said, "and not at the War."

Questions

I was proud of Dad. He was an artist, an industrial designer, and traveled to wherever there were jobs. He told us the reason we had to sell our home and move to Bethlehem, near the steel mills, was because of his work. Grandmother said Dad was born with a pencil in his hand!

Dad, Matt, and I designed our Christmas cards. While Dad illustrated the cards with a Christmas scene, Mom and I composed the greeting and rhyme. Matt folded the cards, stuffed them in envelopes, and put on the stamps.

Mom hugged me, "And we have plenty of love to go around. Now, it's way past your bedtime. Let's say our prayers. We'll thank God for our blessings, pray for peace, and ask for wisdom and guidance."

Mimi's Gift

After prayers, Mom turned on my reading lamp. She sat in the rocking chair next to my bed and took out yarn and needles from her knitting basket. Mom was knitting me a red and white striped sweater. It seemed like Mom's hands were always busy. "Work follows faith" was one of her favorite phrases.

"Mimi, now we'll do our best. Faith, obedience, and love are required of us. That takes work on our part," Mom said. She nodded her head and smiled.

"I try hard to do exactly what you and Dad say. But I hurt and feel empty inside because I don't have a gift," I said sadly, rubbing my stomach. "What if the kids laugh at me?" I crossed my arms over my chest. "I'll stay home! I'm too ashamed and embarrassed to go without a gift."

"Dear, I know how much you try. As long as you follow God's laws there's no reason to be upset or worried. Let's believe this problem can be solved."

Questions

"But, Mom, how? What can I take? I can't save money to buy a gift. Matt and I don't get allowances!"

Mom stuck her knitting back in the basket. "Mimi, please stop being a worry wart! Put on a smile." Mom laughed. "I have a plan. Tomorrow we can haul our old trunk out of the kitchen closet and you can open it. We'll go on a quest and search through the hand-me-downs and the things I've saved. Who knows what secret treasures you'll discover buried down in the old chest."

Instantly, I threw the covers off and sat straight up in bed. Mom-Cat, startled by the jostling blankets, was now wide-awake and alert. She rolled over, pulled her ears back, and meowed her discomfort.

"Sorry, Mom-Cat," I said reassuring her with a gentle pat. I put my arms around Mom's neck and pulled her close. I whispered in her ear. "Please tell me what's hidden in the chest." My curiosity temporarily chased away my fears.

Mimi's Gift

Mom saved practically everything. Newspapers, old metal, rubber, and tin cans were saved for the War Effort. Matt and I even collected papers in our red wagon from the neighbors for the scrap drives. But Mom only stored our family's most precious and cherished belongings in the over-packed chest.

The bulging coal black chest, with its rusty metal handles and wooden slats, was scratched and shabby. Inside, the gold lining was threadbare and ripped at the seams. But the chest still held an old-fashioned charm. The curved top chest with its buckled brown leather straps captivated and intrigued me. Engraved on the tarnished brass lock were the initials J.P.N., for Jacob Peter Noble, my Great-grandfather.

Grandmother and Grandpa told me exciting stories about the old chest. They said it had carried books and supplies to the West Indies and Africa and Canada, and to Alaska, where Eskimos lived.

Questions

Mom was a nurse before she married Dad. My dream was to be a missionary nurse and an author when I grew up. I wanted to help people, see foreign places, and write about my adventures! I kept a diary and a notebook where I wrote my thoughts, dreams, and ideas for stories.

Playing dress-up in Mom's old white nurse's uniform, starched apron, and cap was my second favorite pastime. Reading was first! I'd imagine Patience and I were nurses and my teddy bear had a broken leg. Then I'd sit him in my little rocker and wrap his injured leg in bandages. No nurse could ask for a better patient! My teddy bear always took his medicine without complaining, and never spit it out.

Whenever Matt or I had a project for school or needed to make something we couldn't afford to buy in town, we opened the chest. Mom would rummage around in its depths for a while. Finally, she'd look up with a satisfied grin and bring forth some treasures in her hands. Mom would spread the items into neat piles on our kitchen table. Then Matt and I would pick out what we wanted. For some reason, we always found what we needed in the chest and there was always enough.

Mimi's Gift

"Mimi, you'll have to wait until tomorrow to see what's stored away. I think you'll be pleasantly surprised." Mom smiled. She took my white leather bound Bible off my bookshelf, sat back down in the rocking chair, and read me the parable about faith.

"Mom," I asked when she was through reading, "before you go hear Matt's prayers, do we have time for a story?"

"Yes. Just a short one." It was getting chilly.

I snuggled under the covers with my teddy bear and Patience while Mom told me the story about the first courageous, faithful Moravian missionaries, who left home and family to spread the gospel.

When Mom finished the story she kissed me and blew out the candle. "It's late, Mimi. Now, go right to sleep. Tomorrow is Saturday. That's when we'll start the quest for your gift."

"Thank you, Mom." I switched off the light. "I promise I won't ask you anymore questions about the chest. At least for tonight!"

Questions

Although I was wound up tighter than the springs in Grandpa's gold pocket watch, I soon drifted to sleep. Cuddled close to Patience and my teddy bear, with Mom-Cat purring contentedly at my feet. But my dreams were about our old chest and Christmas Eve!

Chapter Two
Morning Chores

Saturday morning I awoke to the grating sound of Dad and Matt stoking the coal furnace, the clanging noise of Mom's old iron pancake skillet, and the rumbling engine of our milkman's truck. From the racket and luscious smells I knew everyone was awake, Dad had turned up the heat, and Mom was preparing our family's favorite breakfast of sausage, bacon and eggs, potato pancakes with maple syrup, and Moravian sugar cake.

I jumped out of bed still thinking about Christmas Eve! Without stopping to put on my red bathrobe or warm slippers I raced to the window to check the weather. I pushed open the blue, heavy lined drapes, rolled up the dark shade, and scraped the frost and ice crystals off the window.

The early morning sky looked steel gray and bleak. Although the wind was blowing and whistling through the bare, leafless trees, there was no trace of snow. I waved to our milkman, Mr. Jonathon, in his green dairy truck. Every Saturday and Wednesday morning he delivered fresh

Mimi's Gift

bottles of milk. He left them in our milk box on the doorstep. A small American flag tied to the hood of Mr. Jonathon's truck waved proudly in the wind.

The cold draft from the window made me shiver and my teeth started to chatter. My fingers and toes felt like icicles. I ran back to stand on the crocheted rag rug by the side of my bed. I dressed quickly in my Saturday clothes. I wanted to get warm by our kitchen stove and open the chest!

Because our family didn't buy many new clothes, I took good care of the dresses I had. I wore aprons to protect them.

Mom had divided my closet into four sections and labeled each part. The sections were Saturday, School, Sunday, and Play Clothes. The hangers in the Sunday area were empty except for a short-sleeved, cotton red flowered dress and the blue coat I had outgrown.

Morning Chores

"Good morning, Patience, teddy bear, and Mom-Cat," I said, smoothing the wrinkled sheets and taking Patience and my teddy bear out from the covers. "Wake up, you sleepyheads! Let's go help Mom make breakfast and see what's in the chest!" I pulled up the blankets and quilt.

Mom-Cat replied with a lazy good-morning meow. She yawned, stretched, and washed her whiskers. Then she followed me as I clutched my teddy bear, shoes, comb, hair ribbons, and Patience and rushed downstairs in my stocking feet.

"Good morning, Mimi," Mom said. "I'm glad you're up. Please put your apron on and take the pancakes out of the skillet. I have to flip the bacon. It's sizzling. The sausage and eggs are on the table. The sugar cake is in the oven." She gave me a hug and handed me my red apron and the pancake turner.

"Morning, Mom." I sat Patience and my teddy bear in a chair and tied my apron at the neck and waist. "When can we open the chest?" I asked. I stacked the feather light potato pancakes on the breakfast platter and put it on the table.

Mimi's Gift

"Not until we do the chores and baking. Dad and Matt are outside getting the car ready and will leave after breakfast. They'll be gone all day helping Mr. and Mrs. Smith, who are members of our church, move into their new home. We need to prepare a basket of food for them."

"Do the Smiths have any girls my age?" I asked hopefully. I slipped on my shoes.

"No. Their youngest son is in high school. Their other son is a soldier stationed somewhere in Europe so he won't be home for Christmas, just like your Uncle Jim," Mom said sadly. "But they'll both be in our prayers. Now, please go and call Matt and Dad for breakfast while I take the sugar cake out of the oven."

When breakfast was over Mom braided my hair and tied red ribbons around my pigtails in perky bows. I tried to stand still and not fidget. Although I knew it was vain, I sometimes wished my hair wasn't dark brown, straight, and plain but prettier, like Martha's. Her hair was red and curly with flecks of gold.

Morning Chores

After Matt and Dad loaded the car, our family gathered in the living room by the Christmas tree for morning prayers. At the top of our brightly decorated tree was a shining angel with golden wings. Dad plugged in the tree lights and Mom lit three of the four candles in the advent wreath, one lighted candle for each Sunday before Christmas.

Cutting down our tree with Grandpa and Grandmother was a family tradition. We'd spend all day tramping through mud and snow at the tree farm searching for the perfect tree. Dad said the tree couldn't be too short and bushy or spindly and tall. But it had to touch the ceiling. *Our tree is special*, I thought as I sat on the wooden footstool by the putz, next to Matt. *All the decorations are either handmade by our family or gifts from relatives.*

While Dad read the Scriptures and prayer from the Moravian Daily Text Book, I held my teddy bear, Patience, and Mom-Cat on my lap. When Dad finished reading, the three of us sang the

Morning Chores

hymns for the day while Mom hummed along and accompanied us on the piano. Aunt Elizabeth said the only way to describe our singing was "loud" and that Mom was really the only one in the family who could carry a tune. But we had lots of fun!

"Mimi, please come to the kitchen with me," Mom said when we had finished singing. She closed the piano and got up from the bench. "I need your help to pack the basket of food."

Mom and I scurried back to the kitchen and filled a large picnic basket with a bowl of hot potato salad, six plump hot cross buns, and a jar of apple butter. Mom also tucked in two jars of canned vegetables and fruit made from last summer's victory garden. Before giving Dad the basket, Mom covered the food with a cheerful red and white-checkered tablecloth. Mom and I stood at the kitchen window and waved good-bye to Matt and Dad as they did their final loading and put the basket of food, an extra snow shovel, and blankets in the car.

Mimi's Gift

From past experience I knew Mom wouldn't get the chest out until we had finished our morning chores. "I'm going to feed Plodder, Mom-Cat, and the sparrows," I said, pouring Mom-Cat's food in her dish. Plodder was my pet turtle. "Then I'll do the dishes."

"Don't leave Plodder out of his bowl. Remember the last time he escaped? We found him crawling in the living room on Dad's brown leather chair. Dad almost sat on him!" Mom laughed.

Plodder spent his day lounging in his large glass bowl. He was a good listener. Exactly the opposite of the two noisy sparrows I had named Clef and Codetta. These two had made their nest in our backyard lilac bush. Last week Dad, Matt and I built the frisky little birds a cozy winter birdhouse.

"Mom," I said, "I need to run outside to fill the bird feeder with seeds." I felt sorry for Clef and Codetta. It was hard for them to forage for food in the winter.

"Wear your warm red jacket and hat," Mom called to me as she cleared the table. "It's cold and the sky has a heavy gray look. I expect we'll have snow before dark."

Mimi's Gift

When I came back I climbed up on the footstool and washed the breakfast dishes. I didn't waste time playing with the soap bubbles in the dishpan. I wanted to get the work over with as fast as possible. While I dried the dishes Mom put the Dutch chicken stew on the stove to simmer.

"Mimi, today is baking day. If we start now we can be finished baking the bread, Moravian Christmas cookies, and Scripture cake by noon." She heated the oven and took out the cookie cutters, rolling pin, and tins. With Mom every day of the week had a special task. "Although some ingredients are rationed, I think we'll have enough of everything we need," Mom said as she opened our "Hand-Me-Down Recipe Book." Its pages overflowed with carefully preserved family recipes.

"What can I do to help, Mom?"

"You can put the whole wheat bread in the oven. I mixed up two loaves early this morning. They've finished rising. Be careful, though. The oven is hot."

"Mom," I said, after I'd safely placed the bread on the top rack of the oven, "let's play a guessing game to make the time go faster. Every ingredient we need for the cake is in a Bible verse. You

Morning Chores

could read the verse and I could try to guess the item and get it out of the cupboard or icebox for you."

Mom agreed. Soon our kitchen table was covered with baking supplies. While Mom measured and separated the liquid and dry ingredients, I whipped two egg whites in a small bowl. "This is easy," I said as I turned the eggbeater handle. "Look, Mom, now the whites look like mounds of snow."

"Good work," Mom said. "You're done just in time for me to fold them into the batter."

After the cake was in the oven, Mom and I mixed up a batch of cookies. She showed me how to stir the dough using her wooden spoon and how to cut out cookies shaped like stars and angels.

"Mimi, would you like to trace your hand on some cookie dough? You can cut your hand print out with a spatula and bake it along with the cookies."

"Oh! That sounds like fun!"

Mimi's Gift

Finally we were through baking. Actually, the time went quickly! But before washing the baking utensils, Mom and I snacked on the leftover raisins and almonds. "Mom, are we really finished? Can we please open the chest?"

"Yes. This is enough work for one day!" Mom replied. She put away the clean tins and pans.

"We've baked exactly one hand print, three dozen cookies, one cake, and two loaves of bread," I said placing the cookies in neat rows on wax paper on the kitchen counter. The smells of ginger, cinnamon, and homemade bread were tempting and reminded me it was hours since breakfast. I glanced up at the kitchen mantle clock. "Look! It's twelve o'clock!"

"I knew we'd be through by noon," Mom said. "I couldn't have done all this baking without your help. Thank you. You've been very patient. Now, let's have a tea party lunch and sample the cookies. After we eat, we'll open the chest." Mom put the teakettle over to boil and made toasted cheese sandwiches while I changed into a crisp, clean white apron.

Then I carefully removed her blue and white teapot and plates from the china closet. I also took out my small blue and white dishes, and put them on the kitchen table. I loved tea parties!

Mimi's Gift

Grandmother gave me my little tea set on my sixth birthday. Grandpa made me a small wooden tray to go with the tea set. I heard Grandmother tell Mom it was important I learned to be ladylike and practice being a gracious hostess. Grandmother never went anywhere without her hat, lace handkerchief, gloves, and shell cameo pinned at her throat.

Suddenly my thoughts were interrupted by the sound of hissing steam and the clattering of the old teakettle's lid. "Mom, your water's hot." I hurried to get her a potholder.

Mom made her tea and I poured a cup of milk for myself. Before sitting down, I filled Mom-Cat's saucer with cream and sat Patience and my teddy bear in my little rocking chair. I sat up straight and didn't sprawl or squirm in my chair during lunch. I used my best manners and tried not to think about the chest or drop crumbs on Mom's hand-crocheted lace tablecloth.

Morning Chores

Mom-Cat, now full and happy, meowed a grateful "thank you" and walked with a dignified stride to her basket, underneath the china cabinet. She curled up on her royal purple pillow trimmed in gold fringe, and purred her contentment. From this secluded spot Mom-Cat had a clear view of the entire kitchen.

"Mimi, now it's time for some fun!" Mom said, grinning. "Let's go open the old chest!" She piled the dirty dishes on our large pewter tray, carried them to the kitchen sink, and stacked them in the dishpan.

"Hurray!" I shouted. "It's finally time to solve this mystery. Mom, I'll help you. It will take both of us to lift the chest!" I hurried to wash and dry the dishes. Then I raced to open the kitchen closet door.

Chapter Three
The Quest

"We can do it!" Mom and I repeated together as we half carried and half dragged the old chest by its rusty handles from the kitchen closet to the middle of the kitchen floor.

"Oh! The chest is heavy and bulky!" I gasped as I let go of the handle. "Mom, are you all right?"

"Yes. I may have to take some things out to lighten it," she said with a big sigh. Mom sank into the kitchen chair. "Let's rest. I'll finish my tea, then I'll help you unfasten the leather straps."

"I can unbuckle them by myself," I insisted. "I'm too excited to wait." My fingers fumbled as I tried to open the buckles. "Oh! I wish I could go faster!" I moaned impatiently.

"There's no need to hurry. Take your time. I'll get the key." Mom stood and walked to the china closet. She reached up and took down the big brass key. It was safely hidden under our mantle clock. Mom handed me the key.

My hands shook as I put the key in the lock. I carefully turned the key first to the left and then

The Quest

to the right. The rusty lock grated and squeaked. The screeching hurt my ears.

Slowly, Mom and I lifted the curved top lid. The smell of mothballs mixed with lavender greeted my nose. Quickly I closed my eyes and pinched my nose shut until the pungent odor drifted away.

Then I gently took out our memory box. It held Mom's and my Moravian outfits. Mom had made them. She said the outfits were a part of our heritage that shouldn't be forgotten or lost. Because Mom was married, the ribbons in her jacket and cap were blue. My ribbons were bright red. Also crunched in the memory box were Great-grandmother's wedding gown, gold ring, delicately carved cameos, parasol, a blue china teapot, and Matt's and my baby shoes.

Next, I removed the old family Bible, bound in black leather, carefully nestled beside the box.

The Old Chest

WORK
FOLLOWS
FAITH

Family Memories

PICTURES
STAMPS

Wool
Thread

The Quest

In the chest we also found:

- Dad's violin and Grandpa's mouth organ;
- old-fashioned ladies' brimmed hats decorated with veils, flowers, and rainbow colored feathers;
- white button gloves, a colorful fan, a beaded purse wrapped in a Spanish shawl;
- photograph albums with pictures of relatives lined up in rows;
- a Scottish kilt closed with a silver safety pin;
- crayons, pencils, and paints in a shoebox;
- my black patent tap dancing shoes and opera glasses;
- a tambourine wrapped in a purple and red flowered skirt;
- Dutch wooden shoes with windmills painted on the toes;
- Mom's old starched nurse's uniform, cap, apron, and cape;

Mimi's Gift

- from the wild west, a cowboy's hat, lariat, bandanna, and vest;
- a silk kimono with flowing sleeves;
- a homemade hand puppet with a raw potato head;
- a carved miniature wooden lion, elephant, and giraffe;
- cans full of foreign coins, stamps, and beads;
- bundles of cloth and hand-me-down clothes;
- boxes of shells, buttons, Irish lace, felt, wool, and thread;
- and old musty books, picture postcards, and letters stained yellow with time, all tied with red twine.

"Mom," I said when all of that was laid out, "the chest is empty. All that's left is a tan camel hair coat trimmed with dark brown fur." I shook my head and frowned. To chase away my disappointment I thought I'd put on my tap shoes.

The Quest

"Stop!" Mom commanded. "Close your eyes. Don't peek or move!" She covered my eyes with her hand.

"Why?" I asked, bewildered. I closed my eyes, stood still, and clutched my tap shoes close to my heart.

"You'll see in a minute! Ready? Now you can look!" Mom was smiling widely as she took her hand down from my face.

I opened my eyes and gasped! In the bottom of the chest, was a partially concealed drawer. "Mom, I never knew the chest had a hidden drawer! Can I open it?"

Mom looked into my questioning eyes. "Yes. Go slow and be careful."

I cautiously pulled open the drawer. Folded neatly in white, crinkled tissue paper were yards of red velvet cloth, the color of Mom's Christmas poinsettia!

"Oh! The velvet is beautiful!" I exclaimed.

Mimi's Gift

"The material has been in the drawer for years. There's enough velvet to make you a dress, Mimi, and the camel hair coat can be altered into a winter coat."

Mom pulled an envelope from her apron pocket. "Yesterday I received a letter from Grand-mother and Grandpa. They wrote to say they have made arrangements for you to have free, private tap dancing lessons." Mom took the letter out of the envelope and handed it to me.

I couldn't believe what I heard and read. Overwhelmed by all this good news I threw my arms open in joy! Then I clapped my hands and tried to shout, but I lost my voice. I was speechless for the first time in my life. I gulped and took a deep, long breath. "Mom, thank you! I love the red velvet, and being able to take lessons again!"

"I thought you'd be surprised and happy!" Mom said with a grin.

She lifted the coat and material out of the chest and held the plush velvet up to examine it. The red velvet rippled and shimmered in the light. "With the old black hat, the felt, and the fur I can style a brimmed hat and a muff for you."

Mimi's Gift

I took the velvet in my hands and rubbed the fabric gently against my cheeks. "The velvet feels soft and the fur feels warm. Now I'll have a new dress and coat to wear on Christmas Eve!" I said, hugging her.

"Mimi, let's see how you'll look in this vivid red color." Mom bent down on her knees. "Stand still!" She draped the velvet around me like a cape and pinned it under my chin.

I scooped up the black-flowered hat and plopped it on my head. Then I pulled on the white button gloves, picked up Patience, and slipped my feet into my tap shoes. While Mom clapped her hands, I danced back and forth singing, "Tap! Tap! Tap!" as I imagined how I would look in my new clothes. Mom and I laughed so hard at how ridiculous I appeared.

In my excitement I forgot I didn't have an offering to take to church. All of a sudden I stopped laughing and dancing. I sat Patience in my rocking chair and unpinned the velvet, letting the cloth slide off my shoulders. The red velvet sank, like my dreams, in a heap at my feet to the kitchen

The Quest

floor. I slowly took off the hat and gloves and my tap shoes, and put them back in the chest. I felt full of despair, as though all hope was gone. I gathered up the velvet, folded it, and handed it back to Mom.

"The velvet is beautiful," I said, "but I still need a gift to take." Overwhelmed with shame I clenched my hands shut and bit my lip. "I'll just stay home on Christmas Eve." I bent my head low to hide my bitter disappointment, hot tears stinging my eyes.

Chapter Four
Patience and Faith

Mimi," Mom whispered, "don't give up! Have faith. We'll find a way." She wrapped her arms around me and held me so close I could hear her heart beat.

Then I saw a piece of new, white cotton material tucked among the hand-me-downs and a skein of dark brown wool peeking out from one of the boxes. I stared at the cloth and wool and smiled through my tears.

"Mom, I have a great idea!" I shouted. I darted from her sheltering arms and scooped up the cloth and wool. "Do you think I could make a cloth doll for my gift? Girls love dolls!" I hurried on. "I'll make the doll the same way that you made Patience. I could stuff the doll with cotton and sew brown wool on for hair." I waved the white cloth and brown wool like flags over my head.

"A little doll would be a perfect gift!" Mom said with a big smile.

Mimi's Gift

Her words reassured me. I regained my enthusiasm and wiped my eyes with my sleeve. "Mom, let's start sewing now so we can have everything ready by Christmas Eve."

But right after I said those words I began to doubt my abilities. My head started to hurt and my stomach began to churn. It felt like there were butterflies fluttering inside me. I wished I had never thought of making a doll or suggested it. *If only I'd learn to be more patient!* I thought.

"Mom," I whispered, "maybe making my Christmas outfit and doll isn't such a good idea. Some of this stuff is just hand-me-downs. What if we run out of material and don't finish on time?" Not waiting for her answer, I mumbled. "Do you really believe I can make a doll? Because I'm still not grown up. Helping mend and darn socks is all the sewing I've ever done. And I've never used the sewing machine by myself."

"Yes," Mom said, "I believe you can make a little doll. I'll help you if you get stuck. Let's have faith. I think we'll have enough of everything we need and some to spare." She continued to sort the mountain of items piled high on the kitchen floor.

Patience and Faith

"Mom," I said, shrugging my shoulders, "if you really believe we can do it, I'll try to be patient and follow directions." My confidence was slowly returning.

While Mom put everything—except the material, wool, and my Moravian outfit—back into the chest, I took the cover off her old treadle sewing machine. Mom kept the machine in the corner of our kitchen where it was always handy for mending.

"Mimi, please go upstairs and bring down my sewing basket. I'll need lots of pins and red thread." Mom closed the lid of the bulging chest, locked it, and put the key back under the mantle clock. "Dad and Matt can put the chest back when they come home."

"After I get your basket will you show me how to cut the doll out?" I asked. "Because I want to do it all by myself."

Mom looked up from adjusting the belt around the wheel of the machine. "Yes, Mimi. We'll cut the patterns out of white butcher paper. You can use my scissors and wear my thimble. While you're getting my basket I'll thread the bobbin."

Mimi's Gift

I marched upstairs to find Mom's basket. My confidence grew stronger with each step. By the time I reached the top of the stairs my mind was made up. *I will succeed,* I thought. *I'll be patient and have faith. It won't be easy, but this is one project where I can let my imagination soar.*

I found Mom's sewing basket in her room and rushed downstairs. "Mom, I've decided to make the doll a red dress. I'll ask Dad to help me draw the doll's face when he comes home." I handed Mom the basket.

"Mimi, that's a great plan! Now, the first thing we have to do is make patterns for you and the doll. Climb up on the footstool in front of the closet door mirror. I need to get your measurements from head to toe. Remember, work follows faith." She took the tape measure and marking chalk out from the basket.

When the patterns were designed, we pinned and cut the material. I was nervous about using Mom's machine. But she guided my hands as I sewed the front and back panels of the doll together. While Mom sewed my dress on her sewing machine, I sat at the kitchen table to work on the doll.

Patience and Faith

"This won't hurt," I whispered to the doll as I cradled her in my arms and stuffed her with cotton. "Well, maybe just a tiny bit. I'll try to be gentle."

Outside, big, sticky snowflakes were covering the ground. The first winter storm of the year had finally arrived! From my chair I could peek through the red kitchen window curtains and see the wind swirl the snow into giant drifts.

Inside, we were cozy and warm. Mom's old treadle machine made a comforting sound and drowned out the howling wind that rattled the windows and door. The fragrance of spicy cookies, fresh baked bread, and simmering chicken stew seemed to be everywhere.

"Mom," I said, "I hope the two little sparrows, Clef and Codetta, are safe. Do you think the storm will continue and they'll close the roads to our church?"

"It's hard to predict the weather," Mom said, still sewing. "We don't know if the roads have been plowed. I'm sure Dad and Matt will have the latest forecast."

Mimi's Gift

Mom's foot on the pedal of the old sewing machine went up and down in perfect rhythm as she sang or hummed the tunes of her favorite Christmas hymns. I also went back to my sewing, singing along with Mom. We liked to sing and make up rhymes. So we composed a little song and called it "Mimi's Happy Angel Song."

Now and then Mom paused in her sewing to pin or iron a seam. During her breaks she would walk over to the table to praise my work.

"Ouch!" I shrieked. "Mom, I'm glad I wore your thimble. I almost pricked myself trying to push the needle through the thick cloth and wool."

My hands got tired and my shoulders ached. But even when the thread tangled and I came to a difficult spot I didn't complain or lose my patience. Mom and I sewed steadily until Dad and Matt came home. We'd worked exactly four hours and twelve minutes. I couldn't remember when I had ever sat still for such a long time.

Patience and Faith

Dad and Matt were cold, tired, and hungry, but they brought good news. The snowstorm was over. The roads were being plowed all the way to our church. No storms were predicted until after Christmas. I was elated! Now all I had to do was to finish the doll and Christmas Eve would be perfect!

Matt and Dad said it was good to be home and out of the cold and that whatever we were cooking smelled sublime! While they dried out their wet clothes and put the chest back in the kitchen closet, Mom and I cleaned off the table. Then we mixed up cheese biscuits, dropped them in the simmering chicken stew, and popped golden corn pudding in the oven.

After supper, I showed Dad the doll and asked him to help me draw her face. "I don't want an ordinary face," I explained as we practiced sketching faces on scratch paper. "I want her to be special!"

Dad steadied my hand as I painted the doll's dark eyes and smiling mouth. He looked down at me, grinned, and praised my art work. Dad hugged me and said I must have inherited the "Noble" talent for drawing.

Mimi's Gift

Matt and Dad took their Scripture cake into the living room. They wanted to have a game of chess, listen to the radio, and play Christmas records on the Victrola.

"Mimi," Mom said as she put the leftovers in the icebox, "before we start sewing again we need to light our welcome candles. I'll light the kitchen candle. Would you like to light the two other candles in the living room?"

"Yes. I'll be careful," I replied. Mom lit the kitchen beeswax candle. Then Mom and I walked into the living room. She watched as I used our taper to light the other candles that were sitting on the windowsills. The light from the candles shone out through the frosted windowpanes into the dark, starless night and glistened on the snow.

"Mom, the burning beeswax from the candles smells so sweet," I said. "It reminds me of our Candlelight Service."

Patience and Faith

Then I resumed sewing, and before I went to bed the doll was finished. "Look, Mom! I'm done! The doll looks like Patience's little sister. She's soft, small, and cuddly. Do you think the girl who gets the doll will love her?" Proud and happy, I walked over to show Mom the doll.

"Yes. You did a terrific job!" Mom said, hugging me. "The doll is adorable."

"I worked so hard to make the doll, I feel she's part of me," I said. "Actually, it was lots of fun!"

"Honey, I'm proud of you for being patient and not giving up. I knew you could do it!" Mom patted me on the back.

"The doll doesn't have a name," I said. "Umm . . . Let's see, what shall I call her? I know: I'll call her Faith! Because making her taught me the meaning of faith. Is that a girl's name, Mom?"

"Yes," Mom answered. "You couldn't choose a better name. It suits the doll just fine."

"I'll wrap her up in a wool blanket to keep her warm. Tomorrow I'll make her a red dress. I'm going to introduce Faith to my friends." I held the doll, wrapped in her cozy blanket, in front of me

Mimi's Gift

and announced politely, "Faith, this is Patience, Mom-Cat, Plodder, and my teddy bear. Now that we all know each other, no one will be lonesome."

Mom-Cat climbed out of her basket, walked over to me, and looked up at Faith. She meowed, and then curled right back into her basket. I sat Faith between my teddy bear and Patience in my rocking chair.

"Mom," I called, bending down to pet Mom-Cat, "are you through sewing my dress?"

"Not yet. I still have to do the sleeves, buttonholes, and hem. You might want to see if you can find some pearl buttons in the button box."

I started sorting the buttons. "This is the first night Clef and Codetta haven't come back to their bird house. I hope they're not hurt or lost. Oh, look, Mom! I found six exactly alike."

"Good work! We can sew three in the front and three in the back."

The chimes from our grandfather clock startled me. Ten o'clock. It was past my bedtime. Matt was already in bed. "Mom, it's late. I'm putting away my sewing. I'll get the broom and sweep the

Patience and Faith

kitchen floor before I go upstairs. It's covered with scraps of cloth and thread."

When I was through sweeping Mom and Dad kissed me goodnight. Then I bounded up the stairs, holding Patience and my teddy bear in my arms. Mom-Cat trailed behind me.

"Mimi," Mom called after me, "I'll be up to tuck you in and hear your prayers as soon as I finish this seam."

On Sunday, Mom and I started sewing as soon as we got home from church. We only stopped to prepare the meals. Mom gave me some scraps of black felt to make the doll a pair of tiny shoes.

After supper, I printed a two-page thank-you letter to Grandmother and Grandpa for "arranging" my dance lessons. I asked them to please come and spend Christmas with us and see me in the Christmas play. I drew a picture of me in my Moravian outfit on the first page. On the second page I drew me dancing in my tap shoes. I borrowed Dad's colored pencils to color the pictures.

Monday was washday. It was cold, crisp, and sunny—ideal sledding weather! Matt pulled the scrub board and our old washing machine out of the kitchen closet and helped Mom and I load the washer with hot water from the kitchen sink.

Patience and Faith

When Matt put on his navy blue jacket, hat, and boots and asked me to go sleigh riding with him, I said, "No thanks. Well, you see," I explained to him, "I'm not doing any sledding until after Christmas. Mom and I are busy with an important sewing project. Right after we do the wash and hang the clothes on the clothes line, we'll be sewing."

Matt understood and even offered to help. Of course, I refused! But I was glad Matt wasn't like Martha's brother, Tom. That boy wasn't nice. He called Martha "Carrot Top!" and sometimes teased her until she cried.

I gave Grandmother and Grandpa's letter to Mr. Sampson when he dropped off our mail. He said Mom-Cat could stay with us until after Christmas. Hurray! I loved Mom-Cat.

Tuesday, ironing day, was dreary and overcast. Mom said we would skip ironing and just sew. That evening we were interrupted by a blackout drill. Afterwards, I didn't resume sewing because it was late and past my bedtime.

Mimi's Gift

Wednesday was mending day. There weren't many clothes needing to be darned or patched. By noon we were back at our sewing project.

Thursday was cleaning and food shopping day. Mom said all we needed to do was dust, mop, and run the hand carpet sweeper. Dad would stop at the grocery store and buy a Christmas turkey on his way home from work. We had the rest of the day to sew.

Friday was Christmas Eve! I got up early and packed my Moravian outfit and Bible in Dad's black leather suitcase. When breakfast was over and the dishes washed, Mom asked me to climb up on the footstool. She wanted to see if the coat fit properly and mark the spots for the button-holes.

While she was measuring with the yardstick I heard the "Clop! Clop! Clop!" of horses' feet and jingling bells. "Mom, it's our iceman!" I yelled. I tried to bend my neck to look out the window and wave to him.

"I'm through measuring," Mom said. "You can take the coat off and go see the horses. I'll get the ice box ready." She carefully placed the coat and yardstick on the ironing board.

Patience and Faith

"Thank you, Mom." I grabbed my red jacket and flew out the door to see our iceman and his two dapple-gray horses that pulled the old wagon. The horses had gold bells attached to their harness. Matt was already outside helping the iceman slide the heavy block of ice off the wooden wagon. They wore gloves and used sharp metal tongs to lift and carry the slippery ice from the wagon to our kitchen icebox. Sometimes the iceman gave us rides in his wagon, or let us hold onto the horses reins and help drive the wagon. Riding in the open, horse-drawn, rickety wagon was fun!

For the rest of the day, Mom sewed on my outfit. As I did my chores, I wondered if she would have my clothes finished in time for church. Faith was dressed and sitting between my teddy bear and Patience in my rocking chair. She had on her new, red velvet dress, tiny black felt shoes, and red ribbons tied around her pigtails. Because I didn't want to forget my suitcase, I placed it by the kitchen door.

Mimi's Gift

It felt like an eternity until Mom finally stopped sewing, looked up from the machine, and called for me. "Mimi, your dress and coat are finished! Come and try them on!"

"Mom, are the hat and muff done, too?"

"Yes. I trimmed them with red velvet ribbons."

I laughed as I slipped my hands in and out of the muff's soft, furry warmth. "The muff looks like the plump, round doughnuts Grandmother fries for us when we visit her." I placed the muff on the table next to my hat.

"Hang on!" I said to Faith, Patience, and my teddy bear as I squeezed Plodder, in his bowl, between them in my rocking chair. "You're going for a ride." I pulled the chair, holding all four, close to the full-length mirror. I also dragged Mom-Cat's basket right beside them, waking her from her afternoon nap. "Now, ladies and gentlemen, girls and boys," I announced, "you're ready to watch a fashion show!" I giggled.

Patience and Faith

A tapping at the window caught my attention. It was Clef and Codetta! They were chirping and hopping happily on our window ledge, safe and sound. "Welcome home!" I yelled, relieved to see them. Then I shook my finger and scolded them. "It's about time you came home. I've been worried sick about you!"

I picked up Faith and carried her over to the window. "Clef and Codetta, meet Faith." I sat the doll back in the chair and hurried to try on my new clothes.

I wanted to jump up and down, I was so excited! But I stood perfectly still as Mom helped me slip my new dress over my head.

"Now, put the coat on over your dress," Mom said, as she buttoned the back of my dress.

I slid my arms into the tan silky coat sleeves. Mom handed me the brown fur muff. Then she placed the brimmed black hat gently on my head like I was a princess and the hat was a royal crown. She held my hand as I stepped up on the footstool in front of the mirror. I was breathless

Mimi's Gift

with anticipation. We both looked into the full-length mirror. I could hardly believe my eyes!

I let out a sigh and clapped my hands. Mom had created a masterpiece of fashion! An elegant winter outfit that had both style and simplicity.

"Oh! Mom, it's beautiful! I've never seen such a pretty dress! Not even in the clothing store downtown. I love how you sewed a red rose and white lace around the bottom of my dress. And the gold buttons on my coat will keep the front closed when it's cold and windy." I held onto my hat with both hands and jumped down from the footstool and hugged her. "Thank you! You're the kindest mother in the whole world!"

Like a model, I promenaded back and forth in front of my admiring audience. Then I turned, curtsied, and blew them a kiss. I imagined they all smiled and agreed it was the loveliest winter ensemble anyone had ever seen.

Mimi's Gift

A sudden blast of cold air from the back door and a loud round of applause surprised me. I looked up to see Matt and Dad, standing in the hall, grinning and clapping. They had stopped their outside chores and had come into the house to see if we were ready for church. After Dad and Matt said I looked "stunning" and congratulated Mom and me on the results of our hard work, they went back outside to scrape the ice off the windshield of our car.

Mom knelt down, buttoned my coat and adjusted the fur collar. Then she stood, hugged me, and handed me the little doll.

"Mimi, your doll is a precious gift of faith, love, and work you can't buy in a store. Never be ashamed to give a gift you made. For when you act on faith, and give with love, you and the gift become one." She put her hands on my shoulders and looked deep into my eyes. "Mimi, always remember: Work follows faith."

"Mom, thank you again for my Christmas outfit. But the best part is I have a special gift, the doll, to take to church as my offering."

Chapter Five
Merry Christmas!

T he chimes from our grandfather clock woke me up. One, two, three, four, five, six. Six A.M. on Christmas morning! *Everyone must still be asleep*, I thought, because the only sound I could hear was Mom-Cat purring loudly at the bottom of my bed. I stretched and snuggled back under my wool blankets and down quilt with Patience and my teddy bear, and thought about last night's excitement.

Christmas Eve was a joyful memory!

I wore my new winter outfit to church. The girls in my class said I looked "pretty!"

When I showed my teacher the doll, she complimented me for making an original and unique gift. All the girls liked the doll and I let them take turns holding her.

"The doll's name is Faith," I explained proudly as our class filed into the sanctuary. "I made her by myself. Actually, my mom and dad helped me with the hard parts."

Mimi's Gift

Burning beeswax candles were sitting on the windowsills and a large, lighted Moravian Star hung from the ceiling. The Christ Child's crib and the box to collect the toys were under the lighted star. To the right of the wooden crib stood a towering evergreen tree. On the other side of the crib the Advent wreath rested on a small table. The light from the star and the candles sent a soft, inviting glow throughout the sanctuary.

While I sat quietly with my class in the church pew, I thought about the girl who would receive Faith. I wondered if she dreamed of having a doll as much as I had before Mom had made Patience for me.

Suddenly I had an idea! I asked my teacher for a pencil and paper. "My name is Faith," I wrote. "I need a home and a girl to love." I folded the note and stuck it in the pocket of the doll's dress.

Finally it was time for our class to go up front with our gifts. I was second in line. When it was my turn, I kissed Faith and kneeled by the side of the crib. I felt happy as I laid the doll lovingly in the crib.

Mimi's Gift

Then I hurried to my classroom to change into my Moravian outfit. I wanted to be ready on time.

During the play, I didn't make any mistakes. I raised my voice and talked loud so that Mom, Dad, and Matt could hear me. They had to sit in the last pew because the church was full. When I glanced toward the back of the church I saw Grandpa and Grandmother sitting next to Mom and Dad. I was glad and excited to see them!

After the Candlelight Service, Mom and Dad said they were proud of me. Grandpa and Grandmother hugged me. Grandmother gave me a bouquet of red roses and said I looked like a real old-fashioned Moravian girl. Grandpa and Dad said they heard me just fine. Mom looked beautiful and delighted as she told me Grandpa and Grandmother would stay with us until after Christmas.

While Dad, Mom, Grandmother, and Grandpa stood by the church door and greeted visitors and friends, I packed my Bible and Moravian outfit in the suitcase.

Merry Christmas!

Dad said Matt and I could ride home in Grandpa and Grandmother's old, gray car. The back of it had an open rumble seat. Matt and I climbed into the rumble seat and bundled up with a sheepskin blanket. The cold, crisp night air stung my cheeks and the whistling wind whipped my pigtails back and forth as Grandpa's car went bumpety-bump over the graveled roads. I held onto my brimmed hat with one hand and slipped the other into my fur muff. Grandpa rolled his window down and yelled back to us that it felt like snow. Grandmother started singing Christmas carols. Matt and I sang along.

When we got home we had a snack of Moravian Christmas cookies and milk. Then Grandmother told us a story about the Moravian Star.

Before heading to bed, Matt and I hung our stockings on hooks by the Christmas tree. My stocking was red. Matt's was bigger and navy blue. On our way upstairs Matt and I stopped to blow out the candles on the living room windowsills.

Mimi's Gift

"Look," I exclaimed. "It's snowing!" Soft, gentle flakes twinkled and swirled like flickering fireflies in the golden moonlight.

But that was last night! Now it was Christmas morning and time to see if anyone else was awake, and put my gifts under the tree. Having Grandpa and Grandmother with us would make this Christmas extra special.

I pulled my hand out from beneath the warm blankets and reached over my teddy bear and Patience to turn on my lamp. My hand bumped against something hard on my pillow. It was a Christmas present! Wrapped in red and white—candy-striped—paper, tied with a big red bow.

"Oh! Where did this come from?"

I rubbed my eyes and pinched myself to make sure I wasn't dreaming: I wasn't! I sat up, startling Mom-Cat, who "meowed" her annoyance. Printed on the top of the present, next to the elaborate bow, was this note:

Merry Christmas!

To Mimi,

Please open this gift right away. Don't delay!

Then when you find the treasure hiding inside,

please join the rest of the family downstairs by the tree.

Love, Mom and Dad

Mom or Dad must have put the gift on my pillow last night while I was sleeping. My curiosity demanded I follow their instructions. I carefully untied the large bow and unwrapped the gift. It looked like one of Dad's big shoeboxes. *Well,* I thought, *Dad and Mom know I need new school shoes. They probably couldn't find a smaller box for my shoes.* I quickly opened the box.

Nestled inside, surrounded by red Christmas paper, was a miniature, wooden, coal-black chest with metal handles and a brass lock and key. It looked exactly like our old chest except my initials were inscribed on the center brass lock. I took the small chest out of the box and sat it on my lap.

Mimi's Gift

Then I slowly unlocked the chest with the tiny key. I cautiously lifted the curved top lid and peeked inside.

"I can't believe it!" I whispered shaking my head. "Oh! I just can't believe it!"

Mom had lined the black chest with sunny yellow velvet. Tucked in the chest and resting on a cross-shaped, white taffeta pillow—trimmed in ivory, hand-crocheted lace—was a flat, radiant, gold cross attached to a long, gold chain.

Next to the cross was an envelope. My hands trembled as I lifted the bright, sparkling cross off the pillow. The cross was beautiful! I couldn't wait to put it on and wear it with my new Christmas dress! And to thank Mom and Dad.

They must have worked at night, when I was sleeping, to secretly make the little jewelry chest. I laid the glittering cross back on the pillow and ripped open the sealed envelope. A silver framed, miniature portrait of Great-grandmother, wearing this same gold cross, was in the envelope and a letter from Mom and Dad.

Merry Christmas!

Dear Mimi,

This gold cross belonged to Great-grandmother Noble.

She wanted you to have it on your ninth Christmas.

And if you look closely you may be able to see,

engraved on the back of the cross,

the words that will give substance to your God-given dreams.

Merry Christmas!

Love, Mom and Dad

I put the small, oval portrait of Great-grandmother and the letter back in the chest. I slipped the gleaming cross around my neck and carefully closed the clasp. I loved my gold cross, Great-grandmother's picture, and the miniature chest. The day had just begun, but already it was the

Merry Christmas!

happiest Christmas I'd ever had in my whole life!

"Wake up Patience, teddy bear, and Mom-Cat," I said. "Merry Christmas!" I gave each one a hug. Then I sat them in a row on my pillow at the head of my bed.

"Look!" I said, holding the brilliant cross up to the light. "I found the treasure!" The shiny gold cross sparkled and glowed in the lamplight. "And I can see the engraving. The words on the cross are 'WORK FOLLOWS FAITH!'"

❄ ❄ ❄

Now faith is the substance of things hoped for, the evidence of things not seen.

Hebrews 11:1

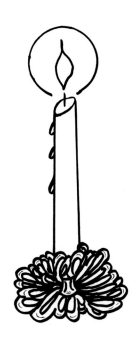

Mimi's Happy Angel Song

Mimi's Happy Angel Song

Second verse:

Angels watching over me all day

Silver wings in the sun's rays

And if you listen real still

You can hear the angels sing

As they gather round about in a ring.

Third verse:

Angels watching over me all day

Teaching me how to pray

And if you listen real still

You can hear the angels sing

Of the love Baby Jesus brings.

Fourth verse:

Angels watching over me all day

Guiding me on my way

And if you listen real still

You can hear the angels' song

As they teach me right from wrong.

Fifth verse:

Angels watching over me all night

Till I wake in the morning light

And if you listen real still

You can hear the angels sing

Praises to our Faithful King.

To order additional copies of

MIMI'S GIFT

Visit our web site at

www.mimisgift.com

OR

Please contact:
Topline NW Distributing
P.O. Box 98633
Des Moines, WA 98198
Phone: (206) 878-9415   Fax: (206) 878-9408
www.toplinenwdistributing.biz

For autographed copies of Mimi's Gift,

Please contact:

Joan M. Thomas
P.O. Box 13063
Des Moines, WA 98198
Phone: (206) 824-3807